DC SUPER-PETS!

DC Super-Pets! Origin Stories are published by
Stone Arch Books
A Capstone Imprint
1710 Roe Crest Drive
North Mankato, MN 56003
www.mycapstone.com

STAR38956

Cataloging-in-Publication Data is available at the Library of Congress website.
ISBN: 978-1-4965-5138-2 (library binding)
ISBN: 978-1-4965-5142-9 (paperback)
ISBN: 978-1-4965-5146-7 (eBook)

Summary: Even Batman needs a crime-fighting canine by his side. But how did Ace become
the Dark Knight's loyal Bat-Hound? Discover the origin of this superpowered Super-Pet in the
this action-packed, POW!-WHAM!-BOOM! book for early readers.

Designed by Bob Lentz

Printed and bound in the United States of America.
010372F17

ACE!

The Origin of Batman's Hound

by **Steve Korté**
illustrated by **Art Baltazar**
Batman created by **Bob Kane** with **Bill Finger**

STONE ARCH BOOKS
a capstone imprint

EVERY SUPER HERO NEEDS A
SUPER-PET!

Even Batman!
In this origin story, discover
how Ace the Bat-Hound
became the Dark Knight's
loyal hound . . .

VROOOM!

Inside the Batmobile, the Dynamic Duo patrol a Gotham City park.

"Stop!" Robin suddenly shouts.

The Boy Wonder points at a nearby river. "Look, Batman!" he says. **"That dog is sinking!"**

FWOOSH!

The Dark Knight leaps into the river and pulls the dog to shore.

"Can we keep him?" Robin asks.

"Just until we find his owner, Robin." Batman smiles at the happy mutt.

In the Batcave, Batman and Robin remove their masks. Underneath, they are Bruce Wayne and Dick Grayson.

"I placed the dog's picture in the newspaper," Bruce tells his partner.

"I'll be sorry to see him go," says Dick, petting his new friend.

The next day, the police alert the heroes to a robbery at a paper warehouse.

ZOOM! They speed out of the Batcave!

"The dog is following us," Batman says.

"It's too late to take him back," says Robin. **"Let's bring him along!"**

"If anyone recognizes him, our secret identities will be revealed," Batman says.

"I'll fix that!" Robin wraps a black mask around the dog's face.

"Nice work!" Batman says.

Moments later, the Batmobile arrives at the paper warehouse.

Batman, Robin, and the masked dog rush into the building. They discover six crooks stealing boxes of paper!

The Dynamic Duo fling their Batarangs and knock two crooks to the floor.

While others get away, the masked mutt chomps onto the sleeve of a third thief.

CRUNNNNCH!

"Yeow!" yells the crook. "Let go of me, you . . . you Bat-Hound!"

"Bat-Hound!" Robin says. "The perfect name for a canine crime fighter!"

"BARK! BARK!" The dog agrees.

Later at Wayne Manor, Bruce gets a call about the dog's picture in the newspaper.

"His name is Ace!" says the caller. "He belongs to a man named John Wilker, who disappeared two days ago."

Along with Ace, the heroes rush to Wilker's home. Inside, they find broken dishes and furniture.

"A fight took place here!" Batman says.

Robin finds a business card. "Wilker owns a local printing company," he says.

FWOOOOOSH!

Inside the Batmobile, the super heroes speed through the streets of Gotham City.

"Woof! Woof!" The Bat-Hound barks as they pass the Gotham Ink Company.

"More crooks, boy?" Robin asks Ace.

"Let's find out!" Batman suggests.

When the Batmobile stops, Ace leaps out and sprints into the building. Batman and Robin follow close behind.

Inside, the heroes discover Mr. Wilker, tied up. He is surrounded by the three crooks who escaped them before.

"Don't come closer!" warns a crook.

Batman and Robin slowly back away.

Suddenly, Ace charges at the crooks.

One of them dumps a barrel of ink onto the floor in front of the dog. SPA-LOOSH!

The Bat-Hound slips on the ink and tumbles through an open door. Another crook quickly locks door behind him.

Then the crooks turn to the heroes.

"If you want Wilker to go free," says one
of them, **"you'll come with us."**

The crooks tie up Batman and Robin
without a fight.

Moments later, they arrive at Wilker's printing company. Inside, the Dynamic Duo spot the stolen paper and ink.

"Lock Batman and Robin in the back room," one thief orders the others. Then he turns toward Mr. Wilker. **"And you, start printing our fake money!"**

Inside the room, the heroes struggle to free themselves.

"I have an idea!" Batman says.

THWACK! He kicks over a lamp. The light shines through a nearby window.

"Now remove a Batarang from my Utility Belt," Batman tells Robin, "and place it on top of the lamp.

"You got it!" Robin follows the direction.

Suddenly, a circle filled with a bat-shaped shadow shines into the night sky.

"A Bat-Signal!" Robin cries out.

Back at the ink company, Ace the Bat-Hound spots the signal.

"Woof! Woof!" He knows Batman and Robin are in trouble.

CRAAAAASH!

Ace smashes through a window and races toward Wilker's printing company.

Moments later, Ace sneaks inside the printing company and sniffs out the Dynamic Duo.

CHOMP! The crafty canine chews the ropes that bind the Boy Wonder.

"Attaboy!" Robin exclaims. **"Once I'm free, I can untie Batman!"**

Seconds later, the Dynamic Duo and the Bat-Hound burst out of the room.

"Batman! Robin!" shout the crooks.

"And that doggone dog!" one adds.

"WOOF! WOOF!" Ace barks.

With the Bat-Hound's help, Batman and Robin take down the thieves!

Mr. Wilker hugs Ace. "I missed you!"

"Woof! Woof!" Ace agrees.

Mr. Wilker turns to the heroes. "You saved my life," he says, "and brought back my dog. How can I repay you?"

"If Ace ever wants to be a Bat-Hound again, the job is his," Robin says.

"I travel for work," says Mr. Wilker.
"Could he stay with you during my trips?"

Ace leaps up on Robin and licks his face.

SLUUURRRP!

"We'd be honored to have Ace on our team!" Batman exclaims.

Back in the Batcave, Batman and Robin create a series of high-tech gadgets for their new pet partner.

They build Ace his own Utility Collar full of crime-fighting tools, including Batarangs, a Batrope, and glider wings.

Ace quickly puts the weapons and gadgets to good use!

He takes down the Joker's pet hyenas — Crackers and Giggles — and the Penguin's Bad New Birds.

On quiet evenings, nothing makes Ace happier than curling up near his friends in front of Wayne Manor's fireplace.

But when the Bat-Signal shines in the sky, Batman and Robin know that they can count on their loyal Super-Pet.

Thanks to Ace the Bat-Hound, the Dynamic Duo is now a **Terrific Trio!**

ACE!

REAL NAME:
Ace

SPECIES:
German shepherd

BIRTHPLACE:
Gotham City

HEIGHT:
2 feet, 3 inches

WEIGHT:
82 pounds

Super Hero Owner:
BATMAN

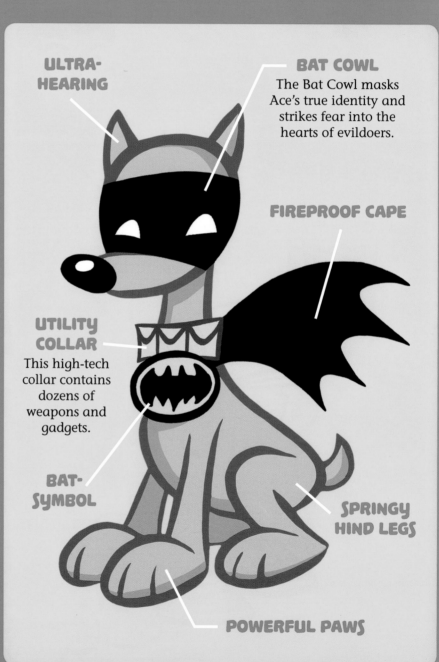

ULTRA-HEARING

BAT COWL
The Bat Cowl masks Ace's true identity and strikes fear into the hearts of evildoers.

FIREPROOF CAPE

UTILITY COLLAR
This high-tech collar contains dozens of weapons and gadgets.

BAT-SYMBOL

SPRINGY HIND LEGS

POWERFUL PAWS

HERO PET PALS!

ROBIN ROBIN

Super Hero Owner:
ROBIN

BATCOW

Super Hero Owner:
BATGIRL

HALEY

Super Hero Owner:
NIGHTWING

SHADOW

Super Hero Owner:
BATWOMAN

COPPER

Owner:
ALFRED

GUMSHOE

Owner:
JIM GORDON

VILLAIN PET FOES!

GIGGLES & CRACKERS

Super-Villain Owners:
JOKER & HARLEY QUINN

ARTIE PUFFIN

Super-Villain Owner:
PENGUIN

ROZZ

Super-Villain Owner:
CATWOMAN

OSITO

Super-Villain Owner:
BANE

LEFTY

Super-Villain Owner:
TWO-FACE

DOGWOOD

Super-Villain Owner:
POISON IVY

ACE JOKES!

What animal keeps the best time?
A watch dog!

What breed of dog does Dracula have?
A bloodhound!

What do you call a great dog detective?
Sherlock Bones!

GLOSSARY!

Batarang (BAT-uh-rang)—a metal, boomerang-like weapon used by Batman

gadget (GAJ-it)—a small tool that does a specific job

honored (ON-urd)—proud of an opportunity

identity (eye-DEN-tuh-tee)—the name of a person; who someone is

loyal (LOI-uhl)—firm in supporting or faithful

patrol (puh-TROHL)—the action of driving around an area for observation or guard

revealed (ri-VEELD)—made known to others

READ THEM ALL!

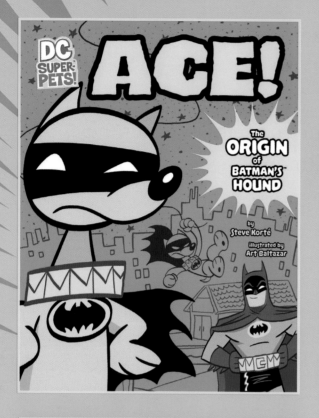

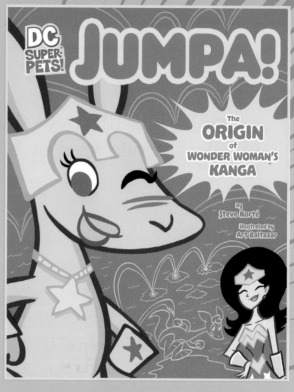